The Deeds of the Ariane Novellas #1

# Lark's Quest: The Search

## BARBARA COOL LEE

*Welcome to the Silver Isle.*

*Barb Cool Lee*

# The Deeds of the Ariane Novellas

## Lark's Quest:

#1: The Search
#2: The Secret
#3: The Choice

## Kestrel Rising:

#4: Raven's Dilemma
#5: Lark's Exile
#6: Kestrel's Flight

# Dedication

As always, for Mom, my co-writer. ☺

# I

A quest. All the old tales began with a quest.

The mild-mannered nobody seeks the sacred toenails of the mystical hedgehog because the gods demand it.

As Lark recalled, the mild-mannered nobody's reward for this was usually enlightenment or great fortune.

Her reward so far had been two chicken heads won in a tessera game, and a hole in her best boots.

She was feeling less mild-mannered by the minute.

"I've seen him," said the grizzled old peasant. Of course he was old and grizzled. The last seven she had questioned had been old and grizzled, though she had enjoyed a spate of young and fair before that. This one had never been fair, and she was beginning to doubt he had ever been young.

"You've seen him?" she prompted, remembering that patience was a virtue, and wringing the necks of the dimwitted was not.

She shifted her weight from one foot to the other. The hole in her left boot made a marvelous squishing sound as her foot sank farther into the mud.

The old man's hut was on the edge of some God-forsaken village two months into her latest journey from the capital city of Chÿar. She didn't even know the village name, not that it mattered. This was another false lead, like all the others.

She hated this part of the Silver Isle. Tall woods crowded in all around, dripping wet and trapping fog beneath the low-hanging branches. The blue silk moths that thrived on this damp coast floated lazily in the still air all around them.

The man's hut was made of the same dark wood as everything in these parts, and moss trailed down from the green-slimed tile roof. The air smelled of ocean and woods and mildew.

She missed the Silver City. She missed sun, and warmth, and dry air on her face. She missed the city's great terraced mountain, its ribbons of green rice paddies framing the intricate canals patterning the valley floor. She missed the soft music of the court musicians, and the delicately spiced food, and the hot baths in sweetly scented water. She must face it: she missed being at the top of the world, both literally and socially.

But this was her allotted task, so this she must do.

She looked down at the old man slouching on his stool, and she pondered again the difference between an abstract defense of the rights of the peasant class and the reality of slogging through the muck and filth and fly-infested villages at one with the common folk.

The old man began to snore.

She prodded him with her boot, but gently, and he snorted awake. His eyes were rheumy, and he looked confusedly at her, as if he had been sleeping for hours, not moments.

"You've seen him," she prompted again. "The man called Raven."

He looked at her warily, noting as if for the first time her glittering silver cloak and the sword sheathed at her side.

"I mean him no harm, Old One," she said carefully. "Do not be afraid."

He gazed through those rheumy eyes at her. "I am not afraid of you, My Lady. You cannot harm the likes of him."

"Really?" She heard the amusement in her own voice. No one was unafraid of her, least of all some unnamed peasant in a poor village. She watched him steadily, and soon enough his gaze broke from hers and he looked down at the muddy ground.

"I will tell you what you want to know, Lady. I saw him a fortnight ago."

Her heart sank. Of course he had no fear for this Raven-named man's safety. A fortnight ago. He could be anywhere by now. She was too late, yet again. "Then he has moved on?"

"Fear not," he said. "You can find him at the sign of the Black Bird during the full moon."

She closed her eyes. She had wasted time chasing yet another myth. "The full moon?" she said sarcastically. "I thought he only appeared in spring, with the new leaves on the sacred Ma trees. Or when the wolves howl in the mountains and the sun sits low in the sky. Or when a girl-child is born on the summer solstice." Dear Lord, she was really trying to learn patience. Really she was.

She opened her eyes. The old man looked at her blankly, blissfully unaware he had ruined her week. She gave him a faint smile and a copper coin that would feed him for a month. "Thank you for your trouble, Old One." Respecting her elders was also a virtue she should cultivate.

She turned her back and started off down the muddy road to her next destination.

She had taken two steps away when she heard, "I always see him during the full moon. That's when I take my crops to market at Rïal."

Two days later, Lark followed meekly behind a young boy as he climbed the path to the cliff above the Black Bird Inn in Rïal.

At the top of the cliff a man stood still as stone, staring away from them, out toward the sea.

"Raven? My Lord?" the boy said when they were only a few paces away from him.

The man remained still, his back to them. His right hand held a walking stick of dark polished wood, which rested lightly on the ground, not bearing his weight.

He was tall, not quite as tall as the pale-skinned foreign devils who haunted the far southern coasts in their great ships, but certainly too tall to have been starved as a child.

His cloak swept the ground in a dark tweed of greyed-blue silk, the color of the fog, or the sea. The muted color and rough texture of his clothing signified that while his class was permitted to wear silk, he was not a noble, but merely an innkeeper. She wondered about that.

Her own outfit was not silk at all, since she now wore the garb of the typical low-caste peasant. Her undergown was of stained, rough-textured tweed, and her overgown was black wool, so old the dye had faded with endless washing into a muddy gray-brown. The fabric was heavy, and smelly, and it itched. The thick fabrics felt unbearably hot, making the sweat run down from her armpits, even though the wind on this exposed clifftop whistled around them.

The wool of her tattered cloak rustled around her. She hated the feel of it. At least the rough-made shoes she now wore had no holes in them.

The mists drifted all around them now, obscuring the view of the water. The boy had told her the man came up here on the cliff every week around this time to watch the fog roll in from the ocean. This time of every week was the peasant God's sabbath eve. Perhaps that was just a coincidence.

Her palms sweated with the tension of keeping silent. Still she watched the man's back.

Despite his clothing she could see he had been of the aristocracy. Even from the back she recognized the type: straight as a bamboo pole, with squared shoulders and head held high, aloof. Ignoring them. Expecting an obeisance, possibly. Well, she would do what was necessary—though kneeling in the wet grass did not suit her. Nor did it suit him, she would guess. She would bet a coin of pure gold this man had bent his knee to few others in his life. She dared not ask herself who may have knelt to him.

His hair was long, and rumpled by the mantle, and must have once been as black as her own, black as the raven for which he had been named. But while her own hair was still black as any peasant's, his hair had turned to a pure silver that on one as young as he clearly betrayed a noble parentage.

From the back it was hard to tell his exact age. If his exact age turned out to be twenty-seven years, three months and—she calculated quickly—eight days, then he could be only one man. And then what would she do?

She rubbed her palms on her gown and waited. Still nothing from him. The torn edges of her cloak were picked up by the wind, and they fluttered around her, making her feel like a fool. She didn't like fluttering clothing. She didn't like this masquerade. Patience was not her best quality, she had been informed on more than one occasion, but she was practicing this week. As she had practiced last week. And the week before. She took a deep breath and tried to act the part of the stoic peasant.

If he would only turn to face her she could end this charade and move on to her next task. Once he faced her, surely then she would know if he was the man she sought.

Her ragged gown was causing an itch between her shoulders. She ignored it. And still the man didn't move. Finally fed up, she made a sound of impatience and the young boy looked at her, shocked.

She had forgotten her place. He was the keeper of an inn. Not a particularly high-caste position, but certainly one that would earn him respect in the tiny, remote village below them in the valley. While she—well, today she was a seeker, nothing more. It was her duty to wait in silence until the man above her station deigned to speak to her. She bowed her head in apology.

"My Lord Raven," the boy tried again. "It is important."

"Yes, My Lord Raven," she said. "It is."

At the sound of her voice he finally turned.

As he turned, his left hand grasped the black-handled sword in a worn leather scabbard at his right side, the swirl of his cloak exposing the weapon for the first time.

"I am busy," he began, but then something in her expression must have betrayed her, for he took a step toward her, drew the sword, and leveled it at her throat.

Quite an impressive display of bravado for a crippled man standing alone at the edge of a cliff, she must admit. She considered commenting on his flair for the dramatic, but she held her tongue.

She was herself unarmed, which under normal circumstances would hardly stop her against one man—but these were not normal circumstances. She had not journeyed through this Lord-forsaken land to kill her quarry. Until she knew if this was truly the man she had spent her lifetime pursuing, all the advantage was his.

So she kept silent and watched the polished blade hover close to her throat.

She didn't look up at his face, but concentrated on the blade itself, praying that her reflexes would be quick enough to step aside before he moved the sword tip one finger-width forward, into the great vein at her throat.

The sword was of plain steel. Lethal-enough stuff, but hardly a rare weapon. It was straight and thin and polished sharp on both edges. A common stabbing weapon. Nothing impressive. Of no better quality than the scuffed leather-wrapped scabbard that had held it. Patience she might not be an expert on, but swords she knew. This was a cheap sword, at least by her standards.

But she noticed his stance was better than the weapon. Though any modest innkeeper might carry such a blade, he wielded it with an expertise that belied his allegedly humble origins.

No one outside a noble castle would have access to the kind of training that allowed him to hold the weapon rock-steady at her throat without the tiniest movement. And left-handed, no less.

No one was trained to fight left-handed. It was bad luck, at the least, and awkward at best.

And yet there he stood, holding the sword from the weak side and looking far more dangerous than any man she had ever seen. She doubted not a moment that she stood an eye-blink away from meeting her maker.

The steady blade, and his cool silence, were oddly calming, reassuring her that he had the weapon well in hand and that the sharp blade was in no danger of slipping.

She stopped holding her breath and took her eyes from the sword to really see him full-on for the first time.

He half-smiled, and lowered the weapon slightly to watch her take in the sight of him.

It took all her self-control not to gasp. She was shocked out of her bravado—not for the reason he must be assuming, but for her own.

Was this the man who had haunted her dreams for fifteen years? Maybe. Good Lord above, maybe.

He was neither too old nor too young. The silver hair made him resemble his father even more than he had as a boy. She ordered her heart to stop pounding.

Other men had hair that paled to silver while still in their twenties. Other men held themselves with that air of pride that made them stand out from the lesser men around them.

But no other man had that face.

True, it wasn't the face she had memorized fifteen years ago. No, his face was not the face she had expected. Though it had been a lifetime, still she pictured a lanky, smooth-skinned boy with a mop of unruly black hair and eyes bright as polished jasper.

This face did not belong to a boy. A lock of his hair half-covered the left side of his face, but it didn't fully conceal the black patch over his eye, nor the thin scar—from a sword?—that ran down that cheek to betray the source of his half-blindness.

Yet even with the patch over his eye he couldn't hide the high cheekbones, the one vivid brown eye looking at her with such cool intelligence. Surely those were the familiar features etched on coins of gold, but rarely seen on a living being?

He held the sword in his left hand, and the walking stick in his right, and waited calmly for her to finish staring at his disfigurement.

She realized she was being rude. And worse, she was obviously unafraid of him. What peasant girl would be unafraid not only of such a scar, but of such a swordsman? She was not playing her part correctly. She bowed her head, and tried to get control of her thoughts. How should she start?

He took care of that for her. "What do you want?" His voice was smooth, and its tone held some barely concealed amusement.

"I want you to stop pointing that sharp sword at me—My Lord." His accent was clearly that of the coastal area, but was there some other undertone to it? Something familiar? Or did she only imagine it?

He smiled, and lowered the sword, seeming unsurprised by her very unpeasant-like answer. "You looked like you were going to attack me."

Attack him. Now that was ironic. "How could I attack you?" she asked innocently, gazing up at him. He was over a head taller than she—and she was a tall woman. This man was definitely not the average bent-shouldered peasant innkeeper.

He laughed. "You had a look in your eye—reminds me of a kitten I once had. It used to beat up my hunting dogs regularly." He sheathed the sword, and the tension eased. "The innocent-looking ones can be the most dangerous." The smile still lingered.

The laugh changed his face. Where he had looked forbidding before—the angular features and aristocratic air making him more imposing than attractive—the smile revealed the curve of full lips, and the sparkle in his eye. She took a half-step closer before coming to herself and stopping.

His grin took in the little boy as well. The boy had kept back until now, obviously wary of the tension between his master and the stranger, but now he chuckled at Raven's joke. Lark wondered for a moment if the child could be his. She hadn't even considered that possibility. A child would complicate matters considerably.

"Isn't that right, Mouse?" Raven rumpled the boy's hair. The boy looked up at him with a frankly worshipful stare. "Now, girl, I assume you have a reason for walking all the way up here...."

"She's here about the job, Master," Mouse said. Master. Not "Sire." That small title could make all the difference.

"The job?" He looked her over shrewdly.

She forced herself back to the present task. She could hardly just barge in here and start questioning him—especially given that he

Yes, praise to the revolution to end tyranny. The revolution sparked by the words of Raven yr Griffon, the king's own youngest son. The revolution that deposed the corrupt old king and set Lady Willow y Ariane the Just in his place as Steward for the dead royal family.

*The king is dead.*

The silver-haired man glanced back over his shoulder and his gaze met hers.

*Long Live the King.*

———

Raven stood aside at the inn's entrance and motioned her inside ahead of him.

The wooden door bore a deeply carved bird, its eyes marked with obsidian chips that glistened in the light of the torches guttering to each side.

The door opened directly into the great room, as befitted a public inn. No screens blocked the view of the main room from the muddy courtyard outside.

As she stood at the entrance it took a moment for Lark's eyes to adjust. The smoky firelight inside dazzled her eyes, and for a moment Raven seemed only a shadow in the doorway, like the dreams that had haunted her for so many years. She shook off the feeling. It was just a trick of the light.

Once her eyes had adjusted, Raven was only a man in a blue-gray cloak standing in the doorway of the inn, impatiently waiting for her to come inside so he could close out the fog.

She stepped past him into the main room of the inn. The inn was dark and smoky after the fresh outdoor air they'd just left, but it was warm, and she could smell the delicious aromas of cooking. The smells made her mouth water after the months of wandering the wild roads of the Silver Isle. Rice cake was nourishing enough, but it wasn't food.

The inn's great room was truly "great," larger than most she'd seen in her travels, and unusually clean, possibly thanks to Raven's noble heritage. Nobility was notoriously fastidious about that sort of thing. Cleanliness is next to Holiness, and all that. The nobles' gods disapproved of filth. Conveniently for them, the nobles never had to do the filthy work it took to keep the kingdom running.

She was no expert in regional architecture, but the inn seemed unlike the other buildings she had seen in this part of the country. Perhaps it had once been the country house of a magistrate. Certainly it was no peasant's shack.

High walls of polished rock rose to heartwood rafters. The swooping arch of the swallowtail roof was clean and tight, with no gaps showing. The floors were of smooth slate of blush red, from local coastal quarries, no doubt. The place seemed old, probably dating back centuries. Certainly it had been built before the birth of the Raven who now kept it.

A long table to one side of the room held bowls and cups ready for evening meal, and she could see the source of the wonderful smells through an arched doorway beyond the table.

The old man who had first opened the inn gate to her that afternoon stood cutting steaks from what could only be a whole roasted shark, with little Mouse chattering away at the man while he worked.

The old man had worn a cloak earlier. Now he'd stripped off the cloak, and worked bare-chested over the grill. Though he must be quite elderly he had the muscles of a young man, and the scars of a warrior.

The man was heavily marked by injury, including one puckered old scar along his temple. She hoped this wasn't a sign he had gone mad.

He looked like a veteran of the first war, when the white devils first tried to set foot on these shores and were beaten back by a band of peasants and Ariane guards fighting side-by-side. That was before she was born. It was surprising to see someone like him; most of his generation had died long ago. But he looked alive enough, wielding his cleaver like it never left his side. He carved at a bit of meat like it was an enemy's innards.

As she watched, Mouse gestured out the doorway toward her. The man glanced up to appraise her with one cold look, then returned to his work. He paused with another glance to be sure she watched, then quickly whittled a particularly juicy slice of fish into thin slices with a frightening accuracy.

She wasn't easily intimidated, but the open hatred on his face brought out some pain from deep inside of her. She felt the sudden urge to turn around, go back out into the dusk, away from this place and these people. To go somewhere she was wanted. But where would that be?

She looked around, trying to see where His Grace had gone. She shook her head. Stop that. She was thinking of him as "His Grace" before she knew if he deserved the title. He was "My Lord" only, until—and unless—he was proven otherwise. She must watch her step.

She turned her back to the cookroom doorway and looked over the rest of the room. A dozen people milled about, talking among themselves. They seemed to be local fishermen and moth-keepers from the actual village of Rïal in the valley below the inn. She had secured lodgings in Rïal earlier today, assuming this visit would take little time. Now she would have to reassess the situation.

She nodded cordially to the peasant folk as she walked past the little groups. Some stood around the table, some sat near one of the two fireplaces at opposite corners of the far wall. Conversation stopped as she passed, and no one did more than politely nod in her direction. She continued to look around, trying to get the layout of the inn memorized, in case she needed to make any sudden moves.

One of the fireplaces along the wall had a single chair in front of it, an overstuffed leather one, not unlike the one the Lady Willow had at the Ariane Temple. It could only belong to the inn's esteemed keeper. But it stood empty, and Lark saw no sign of him. He must have slipped away while she was looking around.

She noticed that no one sat in his chair, though that might only be deference to his status as owner of this place.

She wondered if any of these simple folk held private theories about their host's identity. Certainly they would know he was not from a humble family line—even more than his silver hair, his very bearing made him stand out, though she wasn't sure he realized it. But that alone would not make people suspicious. These were unsettled times, and minimizing one's past was hardly unusual these days.

The question was, what story had he told these people about his past? That would make all the difference, for he could, of course, not tell any lies about himself.

That would be the ultimate test, wouldn't it?

Since the revolution, it seemed half the boy children, and more than a few girls, were called "Raven." After seeing her fifth Raven some days, she occasionally wondered if she would have been better off if he could have changed his name.

But the man she sought was trapped by his own identity. And she was counting on that. This journey to seek out every Raven-named man in the Silver Isle would be pointless if her quarry could have slipped off into the countryside under an assumed name. Ironically, her Raven's royal Griffon name prevented him from doing just that.

Someone of royal blood, descended from the line of kings as old as the land itself, must tell the truth. The taboo was older than this ancient inn, older than the city of Chÿar itself, older perhaps than the people of the Silver Isle. No falsehoods could pass the lips of a royal.

Oh, her Raven could withhold information, he could change the subject, he could parry words with the best of them, his speech's truth balanced on an edge of meaning as fine as a sword. But he couldn't cross the line to a lie.

His words, therefore, carried a weight no other man's could. He couldn't lie.

But she could. She could do all the dishonorable things it took to catch a man of honor. And she would. Because if she didn't, Raven yr Griffon, Lord of the Center of the World, Keeper of the Silk and Water, last heir to the throne of the Silver Isle, and the most admired man in the land, would die uncrowned.

In the face of that, one angry old cook was hardly an obstacle.

She resolutely entered the kitchen.

"I told him you were the new helper," Mouse said. "Raven wants her," he added to the old man.

"I heard you the first time, boy." The man's voice was rough, with the heavy accent of the basest peasant, but the expression in his eyes was intelligent as he looked her over.

"So?" he said by way of welcome. He pointed with the cleaver to a pile of roots on a table in the corner, then turned his back on her.

With a sigh, Lark got to work.

# II

It was later that evening before Lark found a moment to return to the great room.

She stood in the kitchen doorway, dishrag in hand. About a dozen folk lingered in the room, waiting for the food to be served. She wondered how so many could afford to eat at an inn when it was no feast day, but they appeared to be regulars.

It seemed the inn was a gathering place for the locals, since she was sure all of these people were from the village or nearby farms. They all had the look of northern folk, and the accents.

She herself had trouble remembering to put the extra lilt in her voice when she spoke. The more she listened to them, the easier it would be. She knew no one would mistake her for a native of the area, but she didn't want to sound too different: too southern, too educated, too upper-caste.

She wondered what they would think of her. She was dark haired and round-faced like they were, so she was clearly no noblewoman. But she didn't fit in with them any more than she did with the nobles. That was nothing new. All her life she had been trying to figure out where she did fit in. But she worried they could see her profession written all over her—from her walk to the tilt of her head. She tried to bend her shoulders more, to look more meek and humble.

Finally Lord Raven appeared. She caught sight of him coming down a hallway leading into the far end of the room, a pipe of carved bone in one hand and a wooden cup in the other. His walking stick was gone, she noticed, though he stepped carefully and his limp was obvious.

He had shed his cloak, and appeared even taller indoors, with the ceiling of this ancient building only a few handspans above his silver hair. He walked past her, nodding a cool greeting in her direction, but not stopping.

The denizens of the Black Bird greeted him as he passed, most warmly, familiarly, with some deference—he had an air about him that seemed to assume deference, though he never appeared to ask for it. But certainly she saw no sign of intimidation on the people's part, and she grew more certain that he was completely entrenched in his role of mild townsman.

He made his way to the stuffed chair by the hearth, and eased into it just as the cook, little Mouse at his heels, brought platters of shark steaks and rice, and tureens of the seaweed soup for which the coast was famous, and set all on the table to the laughs and murmurs of appreciation from the people.

"Step up," Oxen said, shaking a wooden cup in his hand. The people filed by him, each dropping only one small copper coin into the cup before descending on the evening feast.

The food on the table cost more than old Oxen was collecting. Another clue. So Raven the humble innkeeper fed hungry villagers with no desire for profit. Again like her own Raven would do, if he lived. It had always been his nature to think of the people's needs ahead of his own.

She walked over to the leather chair by the fireplace. There were stares and brief silences as people moved aside to let her pass. Strangers were clearly not greeted warmly here. The barbarian invasions may be far away, but they had everyone on edge. Well, she could hardly be mistaken for a Var invader. She kept her head down in her meekest fashion, and looked over her quarry.

His right eye was closed, and the sight of the patch over the left eye, with the thin scar running in a line from it down his cheek, again shocked her, but she was becoming used to it, and was able to look away after just a moment. His head rested back against the dark leather, his bad left leg settled on a pillow on the hearth, and she wondered if he had fallen asleep, though she thought it unlikely with the noise of the feasters just across the room. The pipe sat near his propped-up leg, the empty cup beside it.

Old Oxen came up, a plate of food in hand.

"Sir?" Oxen said, in a very different tone than the one he had used on her.

Raven looked up. He took the plate with a murmur of thanks, and set it on the stool by his feet.

Oxen raised an eyebrow at her.

"All right. I'm coming," she said, trying not to sound as annoyed as she felt.

Old Oxen snorted.

"Let the girl have a moment's rest," Raven said. Some look passed between them that she couldn't understand, and Ox turned on his heel and went back to the other side of the room to continue serving.

"Tired?" Raven asked her.

"Yes, My Lord."

He motioned to a spot on the hearth, and she sank down. She was glad for the dishcloth in her hands. Her hands felt shaky in his presence.

"You must be tired," he said. "You traveled far to get here?" The question was not idle. He was sizing her up as much as she was him.

"I have no family left back home"—that was true enough—"and I had hoped to find work in the Summer Country. And you, My Lord? Are you from here or somewhere else?"

Raven ignored her question. Well, that was one way to avoid lying—say nothing. He stared into the fire for a bit.

"You've been in the south?" another voice asked.

She looked up to see a young man staring at her. He was one of the fisherfolk from the look of him. Only a teenager, perhaps a few years younger than her. "You're the girl staying with my mother?" His mother must be the tired-looking woman she'd begged lodging from in town.

Damn the intrusion. But Raven turned to face the boy and include him in their conversation, so she could hardly force the talk back to Raven.

"I guess so," she murmured. His mother. So he was some sort of a fisherman. His mother had said something about her son's work at sea when Lark had met her earlier in the day.

"You've been in the south?" he repeated.

"Yes, I've been in the south—My Lord," she almost forgot to add. The boy was no noble, but if she spoke to Raven the Innkeeper as if he were above her class, she could hardly omit the honor for this boy.

"Where?" This from Raven. He looked amused, as if he knew exactly how uncomfortable she was and was enjoying himself. The question was definitely not idle.

"I lost my family to the white devils in Zïl," she quickly improvised. "It was a small town on the coast—do you know it?" She addressed this to the fisherman.

"Yes, I think so." She suppressed a smile.

"There is no such village," said Raven, with an assurance that would have been arrogant if he weren't right.

"Have you seen much of the country, My Lord?" she asked. She plucked at the dishrag as she tried to turn the conversation back to him.

"I've been a few places over the years." He shrugged, and looked away again. He wasn't going to be drawn in so easily.

"Did you see the barbarians yourself?" a woman asked her. "They say they are ten feet tall, with pale eyes that freeze you in your tracks if you look at them."

Lark sighed. "No, they are just people like us—" she started to say, but was interrupted.

"Didn't the Ariane guards protect you?" another man asked. "I thought they were guarding the coastline."

"There aren't enough Ariane to guard everywhere—" she started to answer.

"How long ago was the village taken?" from a third man.

She was surrounded by curious onlookers now.

Raven sat back in his chair and watched her. Definitely amused, though he said nothing. This was not the private conversation she had been hoping for, and she had the distinct impression he knew that.

It was her fault. Her lie about her purpose in traveling had worked before, when she had needed a quick story in passing through town. But here she was a newcomer, arrived supposedly to stay, and she had underestimated these folks' curiosity about her.

With a sigh, she faced her audience of the entire dozen folk all expectantly waiting for her gruesome story of barbarian slaughter.

She gave it to them, describing the muscular, pale Var with only slight exaggeration, and embellishing what little she'd seen of their bloody exploits with every disgusting detail she could conjure. One by one, they blanched and set down their bowls of soup and rice.

Through it all, Raven sat silent and apparently uninterested, except for the twinkle in his eye. She felt like she was giving a command performance—and failing miserably. But she struggled on, caught in a lie and now trying to talk around it to some sort of coherent autobiography that would satisfy, if not the silent man quietly watching her, at least the rest of her audience.

When she finished, she waited for the response.

The fire in the hearth guttered, hissing. The room was still.

One of the men eventually spoke. "What can we do to protect ourselves?"

Raven lit his pipe, releasing the acrid smell of burnt herbs into the air. He stared off into the fire for a bit. Everyone in the room seemed to wait.

"The Var are unlikely to come this far north for a while," he eventually said. "They are finding what they want in the villages closer to their landing points. It is the southerners who are suffering, while we make up the lost tax they can no longer pay."

"But what do the barbarians want?" the man asked.

Raven shrugged. "Our silk, of course. No one in the known world makes silk like we have in the Silver Isle. It is what made this land wealthy in times past. Now the Var seafarers have decided they are not satisfied to serve as our paid couriers to the great Irini trading markets overseas. Why should they work for us when they can simply take our trade goods and keep all the profit for themselves? They have conquered the long sea passage, and they won't be beaten back easily."

"But the Ariane should be able to protect us," a woman said. There were murmurs of agreement from the others.

Oxen moved through the group to silently refill Raven's cup. He stood next to Raven's chair, the wine jar in his hands, looking like he wanted to hit Lark over the head with the jug.

Lark ignored him and looked expectantly at Raven. "Why not the Ariane, My Lord?"

Raven shook his head. "They're spread too thin. The Ariane mission was founded to guard one castle—"

"—And one royal family," Oxen cut in with a sneer. "They couldn't even do that job right."

His words were close to blasphemy, but Raven just smiled indulgently at him. "Relax, my old friend. You will spill your good wine, and that would be a shame. We are safe here."

"Are we safe, My Lord?" Lark asked.

"Yes, Lark," he said quietly, looking directly at her. The look seemed to bore into her soul. He was still a handsome man. No scar could change that. He watched her steadily, and she felt herself blush, and hated herself for that reaction. He had made many women blush, she imagined. He smiled gently, and his voice grew tender. "You needn't fear that the ten-foot barbarians who killed your family in Zil will strike here." He spoke with great seriousness, as if comforting a small child. Very subtle, was Raven the Innkeeper. So he knew she was a liar, and he wanted her to know he had caught her in a lie.

She nodded slightly. "Thank you, My Lord," she said formally.

"But even if we are safe here, don't you care about what happens in the south?"

He looked a bit taken aback at that, but the look quickly passed, and he shrugged. "It's not my concern. I keep this inn, and pay my taxes, and cause no trouble. I am not responsible for the fate of the Silver Isle."

The last sentence seemed to echo in Lark's mind. Not responsible? Shocked, she looked down at the dishrag in her trembling hands and tried to gather her wits about her. He was telling the truth as he saw it. There were only two possibilities.

One, he really was just a simple innkeeper of noble descent who was a bit arrogant in his manner, overly generous to his neighbors, and he could not be held responsible for events beyond his own small world. He was only a man who happened to be the right age, with the right look, and even the right feel about him. And she was so desperate to find her own Raven she had fooled herself into believing this man might be the lost heir of the Griffon throne.

Or else, far worse, he actually was Raven yr Griffon, and he was telling the truth—as a Griffon heir must. And that meant he truly did not feel responsible for the fate of his country.

"But the Ariane—" she stammered, trying to make sense of it.

"Forty-four Ariane guards cannot defend the entire coastline, child," he said dismissively.

Child. She wanted to smack him. She was almost twenty years old, only eight years younger than the missing prince. She was no child.

She glared at him and he hid his smile behind the wine cup.

Then a wave of embarrassment washed over her. Did he see through her disguise to what she really was? No, it could not be. She may not be worldly in the ways of men and women, but he could not know that about her. She knew of the whispers behind their backs: Her kind were women in name only, untouched by men, devoted only to duty. Devoid of feeling.

She felt the blush rise on her cheeks, and hoped her suntanned skin was dark enough to cover it.

"Then why don't we get more of them?" asked little Mouse.

Both Lark and Raven jumped. They had been so focused on each other that the others in the room had disappeared. Lark looked up to see the crowd still gathered around them, and all eyes on Raven, not her.

"Then the Ariane could protect us," Mouse persisted. "They know all the magic in the world."

Raven said nothing, seemingly as flustered as she was by the interruption.

Oxen looked from Raven to Lark and back again, then finally broke the silence. "It's not that simple, boy. You have never seen an Ariane. They are not like any warriors you can imagine—and not just because they're women."

Raven looked into the fireplace again, and Lark thought his hand wasn't completely steady as he raised the cup of wine to his mouth and took another sip. Surely he couldn't have felt the tension between them the way she felt it? She was not the kind of woman who could disrupt the confidence of a man like Raven—whether he was innkeeper or prince.

"The Ariane are raised to their task from childhood," said Oxen. His voice was lifted like a storyteller's, and he stepped away from Raven, speaking so all could hear, and drawing the attention away from his master. Between Old Oxen and Raven, they made quite a pair.

"Noble families offer their baby daughters to the Ariane," Oxen continued in that storyteller's voice, and the crowd turned toward him, no longer focused on the silent man by the fire.

"In the ancient tradition, to be Ariane was considered the highest calling a noblewoman could achieve. But only the best were selected by the secretive warriors. They took the strongest and cleverest of the noble's daughters, and raised them in the ways of the warriors. To this day they never marry, and never bear children, so their successors must be found among a new generation of noble children."

"I've got a noisy girl babe in my house that never stops crying," said one man. "They can have her."

"They'd never take a peasant," Raven said. He stood, as if preparing to leave, and Lark stood also. He was a tall man, she noticed again, and she hated that she also noticed the ripple of lean muscle under his tunic. She had no business noticing such a thing.

"They are the daughters of great families who give up everything to spend a lifetime in service," Raven finished.

In service to the king, Lark noticed he left out.

Raven handed her his empty cup, and she took it. She was his servant, nothing more.

"'Tis a pity they never marry," Ox grumbled. "I've seen a few that could use a good bedding."

"Never try to seduce an armed woman," Raven said with a wide grin. "It makes for a short courtship."

Chuckles all around at that.

"Besides," he said. "I'm not sure I would want a lover with absolute power."

"But—" Mouse started, but Oxen cut him off.

"They can kill anyone," Ox explained.

"Except someone of royal blood," Raven corrected. "If you were a prince, the Ariane couldn't touch a hair on your dainty head, young Mouse." He ruffled the boy's hair.

Old Ox scowled at that.

Again, Raven's words could be that of a lost prince, or a fairly worldly innkeeper.

The conversation drifted back to the plight of the vulnerable villages, and the apparently hopeless task of protecting them. Raven began to move away from the group, apparently to slip away again into the private rooms at the back of the inn.

Lark stepped into his way, and he paused.

"If we had a king—that would change everything." She addressed the group, but Raven could not leave with her barring his way.

There were nods and mutterings from all around the room: "The girl is right." "Aye, that would change it." "If only the king lived, all would be well."

"What good would a king do?" Raven asked. There was an edge of bitterness in his voice.

She faced him straight on. "A king could unite the people—give them hope," Lark said. "It would at least be his duty to try."

"Duty?" Raven said scornfully. "A king has a duty to no one but himself. So says the Book of Rule—and that is the only law that binds a king."

"Not all believe that, My Lord."

He raised an eyebrow at that. She was still blocking his way.

"Those who believe in the peasant's God believe the king is bound by their God's law, little Lark. But to believe the peasant God has sovereignty over the king is itself a blasphemy against your theoretical king." He smiled. "I enjoy a philosophical debate as much as the next man, but not right now...." He stepped past her.

"The king's own son was a blasphemer," Lark said to his back. "Prince Raven yr Griffon said that there is no difference between the son of a king and the son of a farmer."

Raven stopped, but did not turn around. "He sounds like an idiot to me," he said softly.

"Raven yr Griffon said that slaves and nobles are the same in the one God's eyes," she continued. "And that the nobles' obsession with elegant tombs and elaborate burial rites is nothing but empty ritual. The only future is in equality for all citizens of the Silver Isle." She was speaking treason, but who here would report her? And to whom? The Ariane? "The peasant's God says that justice for all is the only way to the afterlife," she finished.

Several of the fisherfolk murmured agreement. "True words," the man nearest her muttered.

"Those who believe that are fools," said Raven firmly, stopping the muttering in the crowd. "There is no god beyond this world. There are only powerful people who take what they want. You either become one of the powerful, or you get out of their way."

Become one of the powerful. That was her truth, but was it his? "What about justice, My Lord?"

Raven looked back over his shoulder at her. "You could go blind looking for justice, Lark—some of us already have." Several in the crowd chuckled, apparently thinking Raven won that point.

Lark took breath to speak again, but Oxen cut her off. "The royal family is dead, Lark. Every last one of them. There are no Griffon heirs to take up the crown. So your blathering about what might have been is pointless."

Oxen picked up a cup and raised it high. "Blessings to the memory of the forever-dead king, and to his entire family." Oxen emphasized that word. "Denied their royal afterlife by the peasant murderers, may they at least lie in peaceful rest."

Raven walked away without another word as everyone else drank a toast to the dead king.

She had heard enough. As the people drank their toast she slipped back into the cookroom.

She took down her cloak from a peg by the back door.

"Where are you going?"

She turned. It was the boy, Mouse.

"Home," she said. "I have lodging for the night down in the village."

"But you can stay here. There is room by the fire."

"I already bespoke the space. She will be expecting me."

"But you are a lady," he said, eyes wide. "You cannot walk alone to the village after dark."

"I am no lady, Mouse."

He shook his head at her and then reached on tiptoes for his own small cloak. "I will go with you."

She did not dare smile. "To protect me?" She looked down into his oh-so serious face.

Though he had been wide-eyed at the talk of barbarian invaders and magical warrior women, he nodded briskly. "Of course, Lark. You cannot go alone out in the dark." He reached for the iron handle on the door and pulled it open. The air chilled her through her tattered peasant cloak, and the night outside was dark as pitch.

She placed her hand over his. "Thank you, Mouse. You are most kind. But I will be safe."

He looked doubtful.

"Really," she reassured him. "I have traveled far alone without harm, and I know the way to the village."

"But—"

She stepped around him through the doorway, then reached to close it behind her, leaving him staring after her.

"You have no need to fear for my safety, Mouse." No need at all.

The closed door sealed off the lights from inside. Only a gibbous moon lit the ground, but it was enough to show her way clearly.

The road from the inn led past a small barn which—from the sounds and smells—must house the inn's chickens and pigeons. The road continued down from the sea cliff where the Black Bird stood toward the lights of the village of Rïal below.

She did not take the road.

A small path meandered left, through the trees. She followed it. Eventually the track faded out, but she kept going, following the crest of the small hill through the forest until it plunged downward into a little tree-lined gully.

Finally she came to a clearing, a circle of young firs sprouting from the dead stump of the mother tree at their center.

She stopped and listened. A gap in the woods showed the gleam of moonlight on water to her left, and she heard the whisper of waves on the shore. Around her the iridescent-winged blue moths fluttered through the trees, going about their silent business. All else was still.

Mist like smoke curled around her feet. She dropped the tattered cloak she had been wearing on the ground, and went to retrieve the bundle she had hidden earlier that day.

Opening the pack, she pulled out her own cloak and unfurled it. It was lined in the softest wool, the gray of a dove's feather, and padded and quilted until it felt as plush as a bed-cushion. But that was not what anyone else would notice. The outer layer glittered in

the moonlight, as iridescent in its own way as the moths' wings. The
silvery metal rings that made up the blade-proof mesh were woven
together so tightly they made a shimmering layer as sleek as silk, and
just as smooth.

She shed the peasant clothing, and dressed in her own clothes.
She moved slowly, meditatively, allowing the feel of donning sleek
silks to wash over her in the familiar ritual. She tried to empty her
mind, though thoughts of the day's events battered at her
consciousness with every breath.

Later. Think later. Now was time for meditation and prayer.

She swirled the cloak around in her one smooth movement, and
as it settled around her shoulders she sighed at the familiar,
comforting weight of it. She clasped the fabric at her throat with the
pale blue mother of pearl brooch that marked her rank. Number Six.
She was not Lark. She was number six of forty-four.

At the bottom of her pack lay the doeskin-wrapped wooden
scabbard. She stood, and belted it to her waist. To be Ariane was to
be only a shadow. No desire, no passions, no fear. Just ritual and
instinct, an empty vessel in service to the king.

The king. The thoughts hammered at her. This man, this
mysterious, captivating man. She felt the excitement grow in her
chest with the thought. She stopped herself. Let it go. Later she
would think of that man, and of the feelings that swept through her
every time she saw him. Now was the time for work.

She sat crosslegged on the ground. She reached up and loosened
her hair, then slowly began to weave it into a single braid down her
back.

The braid completed, she stood. She was dressed in body-
skimming gray silk, carefully knitted by the sisters in the Ariane
stronghold at Chÿar. Her clothes were completely different from
anything worn by outsiders: a slender tunic, close-fitted breeches,
and soft suede boots, all in the color of a pale gray dove.
Unpatterned, unmarked, its very plainness announcing her identity
more than any badge.

She drew the sword with a flash of light reflecting moonlight on cold metal, then swept the sword to point hilt up in front of her. The hilt was plain, unjewelled as all else, simply wrapped in gray doeskin.

As she had every day since she was five years old, she spoke the words of the Lesson Prayer: "Teach me to move without thought, to react before action, to be an empty shell through which all energy flows, for the good of the Crown."

She began the lessons, ritual since childhood. Her body, freed of the stifling dress of the peasant, moved through the exercises, stretching and bending. At first she was slow, feeling each muscle and sinew like an old friend, observing critically the places where she was stiff, or sore, or simply less-than perfect in her form. Then, bit by bit, she began to pick up speed until she became a blur in the clearing.

The sword whispered through the mist, cutting left, then right, up and down, behind and in front of her in the patterns. Her cloak swirled, the Ariane mesh a defense against any blade, its folds a trap for unwary opponents' weapons.

Defense and then attack, attack and then defense against the imaginary enemy; no thought, just movement, quicker than reaction, quicker than any mere warrior. The Ariane were unmatched, above all others.

Soon she felt the familiar sensation of floating, of her body moving of its own will, as if she were somewhere above, watching herself dance through the familiar patterns.

Her senses heightened, and she reached out with her awareness, noting the flutter of the moths' wings, loud as drumbeats. There were twenty-seven moths. Also three squirrels sleeping in the tree above her, their breathing steady and unruffled. A seagull nested in the sand to the west of her. One of the seagull's eggs was about to hatch, the chick trying its tiny beak against the shell.

The seagull's acrid smell was strong in her nostrils, though she had not even known it was there until now. Far off, she could hear a person breathing, somewhere on the path toward the village. He was far away though, and no threat.

She entered the next exercise, shutting out all outside senses to concentrate inward on her own reactions, testing herself against the standard of perfection. Her body was weightless, and the sword was light in her grasp, merely an extension of her own arm as it swept through the mist. She wrapped the cloak close to her body and moved behind the tree, then above the seagull's nest, then back to the starting point of the exercise. Even the gull did not hear her pass by.

Good. The charade wasn't ruining her. She wasn't becoming one of them. She was Ariane. Above mortal desires and petty needs. The feelings she'd experienced watching Raven were just part of the role she was playing.

Her sword glimmered in the moonlight, a thing of eerie beauty, deadlier than any weapon held by outsiders. She was Ariane. She was unstoppable.

Finally exhaustion came, and with it the sweet satisfying emptiness that spoke of work completed well. Her feet met ground again and she lowered the sword to the first position.

Just as she returned to the starting stance for the final time in the exercise, she heard a heartbeat other than her own in the woods nearby.

She moved around, quicker than sight, and came up behind the intruder. Mouse. Damn the boy. He had followed her, and the wide, frightened eyes staring into the empty clearing showed he had already seen too much.

She had seen it herself when she was not much younger than he, and it had changed her life.

Now it must end his.

# III

Before the boy could move, she was upon him, and gripped him by one arm.

"Don't kill me!"

She sighed. She had every right to, but that hardly meant she would coldly murder a child without great cause. But he had walked into quite a mess with his spying, and she would have to do something, quickly.

"You are a witch," he whispered. He made the sign of the peasant god with one hand, to ward off her magic.

"I am not a witch, Mouse. Didn't you hear the talk this evening?"

He looked her over: the glittering sword, the shimmering silver cloak, the magical powers he had just witnessed—but with her long, braided, jet-black hair and wide face, so clearly peasant, so clearly impossible. "But... you cannot be—?"

"—an Ariane? Do you doubt it?"

He considered that, then shook his head. "You flew in the air," he whispered. "You are a magic lady, like the Ariane. But you are not a noblewoman. How can that be, Lark—My Lady?"

A good question, and one with no answer. How could she explain herself to this child when he was right? It made no sense. She was a peasant, a former slave of the lowest caste, yet she was an Ariane, living the highest calling of a noble daughter. It was impossible, yet she existed. She alone in all history had crossed that line from the status of her birth to become something ranking above everyone except royalty. She alone could pass back and forth between the highest houses of the nobles and the lowest slave quarters. Free to travel in any circle, but never really fitting in anywhere.

"It is a long story, Mouse. But we have a more immediate problem. What am I, an Ariane whose work is both secret and sacred, to do with a boy who has broken the law and spied on me?" She gave him her sternest look to shut him up while she tried to think. She could not trust the fate of the Silver Isle to a small child. She tried to think quickly, to figure out her options. She was not trained to show mercy. She had learned in sisterhood, in obedience to her leader, in duty to the Lady Willow. Follow orders and kill all enemies of the king and the Ariane. No exceptions.

Now this little boy stood in her way, looking up at her in awe and fear, with the realization finally dawning on him that—as Raven himself had said earlier—she could run him through and throw his body into the sea, for no one but the king himself had sovereignty over an Ariane warrior.

How could she make sure of his cooperation, without doing what she knew she was supposed to do—but could not possibly do? The Book of Rule for an Ariane warrior said the life of a peasant meant nothing, but she did not believe that. This charming little boy must not die—it was unthinkable. But he must not betray her either, for the consequences of that were even more unthinkable.

Perhaps the answer was right there. The kingdom might hang in the balance of her decision, and he must be made to realize this.

She felt him trembling under her grip.

"I have done nothing! Really, Lark—Lady—My Lady! I did nothing wrong."

"Nothing wrong?" she said softly. "You followed me when I told you not to. You spied on the secrets no outsider can ever see."

"Is it a secret? That dance?"

"Dance?"

"You danced with the sword and the cloak, and you seemed to be one place and then another—"

"—but invisible in between, yes."

"Like magic," he whispered.

"Yes." It had been unfathomable magic to her too, when she was only five years old. She too had seen something beyond her ken, and the Lady Willow had ensured her secrecy in the only way other than death—by making her an Ariane herself.

Mouse could not become Ariane. But awe and fear were still powerful weapons—perhaps more powerful than her sword. "Why should I not cut you down and be done with you?" she asked him coldly. "I have a great mission to perform, and you might betray me."

He took the bait.

"A mission? Of course—you are on a secret mission." The realization hit him, and with it all the excitement in a young boy's imagination. "You're hunting enemies of the kingdom! I will help you. I'm very strong."

Exactly the reaction she wanted from him. She smiled. "I know you are, young Mouse. But you cannot help me—or perhaps you can." She paused. "But how can I be sure you would keep a secret— even a secret on which the kingdom depended?"

She watched him closely. Excitement, wonder, the traces of fear all played out across his face. Finally excitement won out. It wasn't much of a battle for a boy of his years. Curiosity would always win out.

"I will swear it, by all the gods in the kingdom and by the one true God himself even! I can help you on your mission."

She looked around her, then knelt down to meet him at eye-level, dropping her voice to a whisper. "Are you sure? If you tell anyone, it could mean victory to the enemies of the people."

"The Var? They are here?" The fear in his eyes returned.

"No," she quickly reassured him. "Not here. But there are spies everywhere, those who would betray our people for personal gain. You are not one of them, are you?"

"Not me. I am loyal to the crown and the Lady Steward who

holds it for the king's return."

"I don't know," she said thoughtfully. "You are awfully young for so much responsibility...."

That had the desired effect.

He stretched up as tall as possible. "Why, I am eight years old, and I'm very big for my age. I can do it. Please, My Lady."

She paused, looking him over as if carefully considering his fitness for the task. In reality, her mind was racing. How much time would this buy her? Would it be enough?

"Perhaps," she told him. "If you keep my identity a secret for a whole day, then you will prove you can help me on my mission. But you must tell no one."

"I should tell Master Raven."

She had to pause before speaking. "No, not even him."

"He is an honorable and brave man. He can be trusted with anything."

"I'm sure he can. But spies may try to hurt him if they think he knows anything about my mission. No, we must not tell anyone for their safety. Only you and I will keep this secret for now."

He nodded. "I promise."

"That is not enough. Will you truly swear to it?"

"Swear? But I do not have the True God's book here to swear on."

She held out her sword. "We have this." The plain doeskin-wrapped hilt was warm to her touch, and the blade itself glistened in the moonlight, the bands of light and dark metal like shimmering waves across its surface. It was weightless in her hand, though she knew it would feel heavy to one not used to its unique balance. She could feel its power, and wondered if the boy could feel it, too.

He looked at it as if it were aflame.

"Place your hand on the hilt."

"On your sword?" He swallowed hard.

She still knelt before him, the sword between them. "You know what this is," she whispered. "An Ariane sword forged in the mysterious caverns beneath the mountain of Chÿar itself." His eyes were wide. She wasn't sure he was buying this blathering, but she kept on. "This mighty sword was wrought by chosen Arianesmiths to move as quietly as a whisper, to seek out and kill enemies of the one true king of the Silver Isle. It is a sword unmatched in the world. It is not something to trifle with. If you swear on it, you will be binding your life to uphold your word."

He hesitated.

Please. It is this or killing you. Do the right thing, Mouse.

Finally, slowly, he wrapped his small hands around the hilt, above her own.

"I swear it. May I be struck down by the True God Himself if I am forsworn." He pulled his hands away quickly and looked at her eagerly. "Will that do, My Lady?"

"It will have to. Now you have sworn to tell absolutely no one about this, on penalty of death."

He nodded.

With a final admonishment to "watch out for spies," she sent him scurrying back to the inn, then returned to her garb.

The aura of her Ariane status would hold Mouse to his word for a day or two, perhaps, but the flimsiness of her excuse for keeping secrets from Raven would eventually sink in. She must move fast. She no longer had the luxury of time to spend a month chopping vegetables and listening to gossip.

First thing tomorrow, she must have a private talk with Raven the Innkeeper, the "honorable and brave man" who "could be trusted with anything."

⁕

A dancer. Maybe that was it. Raven leaned back in his chair and stared at the ceiling. He pictured Lark in ostentatious flowered silks provided by some smitten sponsor. She danced in a cloud of perfume while soft bells chimed, her semi-transparent gown enveloping that long, lean body while she moved with an effortless grace that brought men to their knees. He closed his eye and allowed the image of a courtesan with Lark's face to whisper through his mind. That easy movement, that little smirk as she teased and tempted—

No. He shook his head, dismissing the image. It didn't fit. Lark had the physical grace of a dancer, but not the demeanor. She lacked the subtlety, the quick efforts to appease and please and cajole a man. He had seen so many women like that in his early life, and always found something uncomfortable about their calculated attempts at flattery and seduction. He had spent years as a target of that desire to use him for personal gain. Lark clearly wanted something from him, but not access to his money and power—since he had none. She was not a courtesan, that he could be sure about.

So, not a dancer. He continued, as he had for the past hour, to try to place this mysterious girl who had sauntered into his life and so thoroughly discomfited him.

The fire in the hearth hissed softly, and he could hear Oxen off somewhere puttering around the empty inn.

He thought about it some more. Something other than a dancer. He knew he had met a woman like her before. A woman with that physicality and economy of movement, that sense of confidence within her own skin, that supreme self-assurance in her own body's ability and power, but with a fire and bluntness completely unlike any courtesan.

An acrobat? One of those nimble little tumblers brought in to amuse the court? It was possible. He pictured her in the sleek breeches of the acrobats, somersaulting through the air to the applause of the nobles gathered to watch. That image was closer, somehow, but still something was missing. Some clue was there that he should be able to see, but didn't.

There was something so familiar about her. Those silken movements, that unconscious grace, even the brash manner. It was all so out of tune with her clearly low-caste ancestry.

He had obviously never met her. The noble women he had met mostly melted into a blur of over-perfumed self-indulgence. The peasant women had mostly melted into a blur of resigned suffering. Even through the sea of faces that had passed through his life, surely he would remember a girl like her.

Lark could be mistaken for no one else. She was something entirely different from all the other women he had known. Something both noble and peasant, though that was impossible. One did not change one's caste. Well, he had changed his, but that was different. She was not hiding from assassins. She was not hiding at all, he guessed, despite her absurd story about her mythical ruined village in the south. She had some purpose in being here.

Was she searching? What could she be looking for? It was impossible she was searching for him, though the old paranoia rose up to make his skin crawl. He had fought the fear of being found for so many years. As Ox constantly reminded him, he was a target of killers who might discover he was the only one of his line left alive. To eliminate him would end the Griffon name forever.

He took another sip of wine. The line would end with him anyway. There was no need to kill him to ensure it. He quickly turned away from that line of thought before it led him into a sea of self-pity.

So, she could not be looking for him—she would have no reason. He was assumed dead, and after so many years his existence would not—could not—matter enough to the peasant assassins to warrant a search through the countryside for him. He had to let go of that fear.

But still, Lark was a question. She was after something. Arrogant, yet a bit frightened somehow. Clearly worried about something, but willing to challenge him on his own ground when it suited her.

A girl like her would not blend into the background. But he had met someone like her, somewhere in the distant past. He was sure of it. She fit a type. But he couldn't place the type, and that disturbed him. She disturbed him. Allowing her to stay had been a mistake.

"Sir?"

He looked up. Dear old Oxen had been working while he sat around daydreaming. "I'm sorry, Ox."

Ox looked pained. He always looked pained when Raven

apologized. It was a breach of etiquette for a royal to apologize to a non-royal. But if he owed anyone an apology it was Ox.

"I was just finished locking up."

"And double-checking the locks, no doubt."

"Of course. And I wondered if you'd be needing anything else."

"In other words, it's late and I shouldn't be sitting here staring at the ceiling?"

Ox shook his head. "Of course not, Sir."

"If you can't say it, Ox, no one can."

"No one can, Sir."

Raven smiled. "But you're the only one who knows that, my friend."

"Yes, Sir."

Sir. That was one of their little secrets. That emphasis Ox always gave the word, turning it from a common courtesy into a substitute for the phrase Ox wanted so much to say, but couldn't: Your Grace. He was so glad he no longer had to hear those endless obsequious repetitions of "Yes, Your Grace," "No, Your Grace," "Whatever you wish, Your Grace" from everyone around him. One of these days, he wished someone would just call him Raven, like an equal. It would be refreshing.

He stood up, noting that his knee had stiffened while he was sitting. He wondered if Lark would be willing to call him Raven. He wondered if he would like the sound of it on her lips.

"Is she right, Ox?"

"Sir?" Oxen put out an arm to help him stand up straight.

"Is Lark right? About the need for a king? The country is spinning into chaos all around us and here we sit—here I sit—doing nothing."

Ox's face reddened. "She had no right to say such a thing. You should have cut that girl down and thrown her body over the cliff," he said firmly.

Raven handed Oxen his wine cup. "Even for you, that's a bit drastic, isn't it?"

Ox shook his head. "No, it isn't. She's trouble."

"Clearly. So am I, apparently. And the idea that people still speak of me, like I could possibly help. It's disturbing to hear people think that way about me—they don't understand how wrong they are. My very existence causes trouble."

"But no one knows you really exist. And no one can ever know, Sir."

"Are you so sure? What if people found out I'm still alive? Would that be such a bad thing?"

Ox emptied the dregs of the wine cup into the fire, and it flared up as the alcohol burned. "It's that stupid girl! Getting you stirred up."

"I am a man, Ox, not a boy any longer. If I get 'stirred up' it is my own business."

"Of course, Sir. But that girl is up to something."

"Obviously. But what? She can't possibly recognize me. She would have been just a baby when—"

"Still, you should send her away."

"What if she's right? What if the prince is needed? What if he could make a difference? My God, what if I have been sitting here doing nothing—"

"—You do plenty enough, Sir."

"What if it's not enough? What if I could do more?"

"The prince is dead, Sir," Oxen said in that firm way he always did. "Need I remind you that the entire royal family was murdered by the peasants Lark thinks need saving? If the prince came forward, he would be killed by those same peasants. He must stay hidden just to survive. What would getting murdered accomplish?"

"No, you needn't remind me of what I—and you—have lost. We have both paid a price." Raven sat back down in the chair. "I am not ready to sleep, Ox. You go on to bed and I'll sit up for a while longer."

"I wasn't going to bed myself," Oxen lied. "I have other things to do." He went back to puttering around the inn, leaving Raven in peace, but staying within earshot. As always.

Oxen had been winning these arguments for fifteen years, ever since Raven had arrived in Rïal, twelve years old, injured, grieving and confused, with only his mother's old gardener at his side. He had barely known Oxen before then, thinking of him only as a gentle soul who tended the queen's flowers, worshipped his washerwoman wife and infant son, and calmly ignored the politics in the castle.

That was before they both lost everything. In the last fifteen years Oxen had become as single-minded as an Ariane—"throw her off the cliff" he said, and meant it. The queen's quiet gardener would never have uttered such a thing. But things had changed—they all had changed—since the massacre.

By the time Raven had recovered—and grown up—enough to really assert his own opinions, Oxen had created a new life for them. He had set them both up in the village with new, fake identities: Oxen was a widower (which was true enough, though the how and why of it was never spoken about to anyone), and Raven was supposedly Ox's nephew, and the illegitimate son of a noble in the south. Few seemed to doubt the stories—and a glare from old Oxen had silenced the occasional questions. Raven needed to say nothing, but just stayed silent and let Oxen do all the explaining. Soon Raven fitted into the role of a young peasant, and Oxen had sold a few of the royal jewels to purchase of the Black Bird Inn. ("We can't have you doing menial work, Master Raven. An innkeeper is a good profession for a man who is not from a noble family, but, shall we say, is not a poor man neither.")

Oxen thought of everything. If the work was occasionally hard, at least it was not unpleasant, and with Ox for company and the superficial friendship of people who liked him but did not truly know him, he had been mostly content. He had been lonely without anyone to talk openly to—but when had he not been lonely?

Occasionally he would consider a different path, or even suggest that he should return to the city and see justice done, but Ox quickly silenced him with reminders of the horror he had left behind. If Raven didn't know Ox could be trusted implicitly, he might have thought the old man was manipulating him, but he eventually accepted that Ox was driven by an overwhelming desire to protect him, and he let go of his old life.

And now this girl was bringing it all back....

There was a knock at the door.

Ox drew his short knife from his belt. "Get to the back rooms, Your Grace, quick!"

Raven sat where he was and raised his eyebrow. "Is Mouse inside, Ox?"

Ox lowered his knife. He opened the door a crack, weapon at the ready.

Little Mouse slipped in the small opening.

"Are you all right, Mouse?" Raven asked. The boy looked shaken.

"I—I was locked out," he said softly.

"Serves you right running around the countryside after dark when there are floors still to be swept," Ox muttered, sheathing his knife and rebolting the door.

Mouse's gaze darted around the room, as if he were seeing monsters in every corner.

"Did something frighten you outside?" Raven asked.

The boy jumped. "Sir?"

"Is something bothering you, son? Would you like to tell me about it?"

He paused, then shook his head. "No, Master Raven. I have nothing to tell you."

Lark's peasant boots clumped along the cobblestones of Rïal. Lord, sometimes she hated being a peasant, and the clunky clothing was the least of it. The village smelled of peat smoke and pigs, and the buildings sat hunched in the darkness, an occasional feeble light showing from within. The tiled roofs continually dropped dampness on the narrow, filthy street at her feet.

As she plodded through the winding street to her lodgings she tried to think of what she would do next. She had handled this whole situation poorly—blundering in without a real plan, so convinced this was another dead end on her journey that she hadn't contemplated how she would approach this man, this Raven, if he were the Raven.

Perhaps she was wrong, she tried to convince herself. She had been wrong before. Many times. The Lady Willow had allowed her to go on these searches for years, and every trip had ended with her returning to Chÿar in defeat—weary, disheartened, and convinced that the long-ago, muddled glimpse of a boy fleeing through the smoke of the castle fire had been only a dream. Ashamed at her failure, she would settle back into the routine of Ariane life, and vow never to leave again.

But then after some time had passed, the Lady would encourage her to believe in herself and her quest—and Lark would realize how stifling the Ariane quarters had become, and how boring the routine, and how petty the jockeying for rank and favor among the Sisters. Off again she would go into the countryside, with a promise to the Lady Willow that this time she would not fail.

And this time? Would she fail? She hated the thought of returning to Chÿar in defeat yet again. The sneers of the Sisters at her failure, the look of disappointment on the Lady Willow's face, the mumbled excuses she always made to cover her own shame.

But not this time. This Raven must be the one. He must. Was she a fool to think the room grew brighter when he was in it? That was no proof. But in all these years, she had never met a man who seemed so right.

There had been that one, she reminded herself sternly. A young man several years ago who turned out to be the bastard son of a local nobleman. It had taken her two weeks to find out his true identity, and she had needed every skill at lying she possessed to get out of there without causing a political scandal when she mistakenly questioned the nobleman's wife about her husband's mistress.

But this time, would it be different?

She finally came to the door of the peasant home at the far end of the village. "Space available" was printed in simple peasant symbols on a sign in the front window, though the character for "space" was crooked, making it look more like the sign read "nausea available." She hoped it wasn't prescient.

She pushed open the door and went inside.

---

She found her landlady sitting with her feet up by the fire. She was sewing on a very worn tunic by the soft golden light of the flames: "My boy, he's always wearing holes in things," she said with a smile.

She motioned to a cushion by the fire.

Lark shook her head. "No, that's all right," she said, but the woman insisted.

"You'll be cold after walking all the way down the hill," she said.

Lark was roasting in the heavy woolen garb after her practice and the scare with Mouse, actually, but she nodded politely and took the seat offered, dropping her pack by her feet. The fire felt hot on her back.

The woman sat back on her stool and watched her with bright black eyes. She was short and round, with a perpetually pleasant expression on her little moon-face. Appropriately enough, her name was Moon.

Lark watched Moon work on the tunic for a bit, enjoying the moment of peacefulness as the needle moved efficiently in and out of the fabric, while the smoke of the fire curled gently up to the hole in the cottage's roof, and mist dripped down from the hole back onto the fire, making it hiss softly.

"I am glad you aren't lost," the woman finally said.

Lark pulled out of her reverie. "Lost?"

"When my son got here from the inn and you still weren't here, he went out looking for you. Lucky you didn't land in a ditch, eh?"

Lark straighted up, all the tension back in her body. "Yes, lucky. I did get lost," she said quickly, "but I'm fine now. And I can pay you for my lodging," she added to change the subject.

"Aye, I knew you would be paying. You got the job, then?"

Lark nodded. The garb she carried in her pack was worth more than the house she sat in, and she had enough gold coins sewn into the lining of the pack to buy the whole village, but she had felt it unwise to appear too prosperous when she had arrived in town this afternoon. So now, she pulled out a handful of cheap coins from a pouch at her waist and, with apparent reluctance to part with them, handed them to the woman.

The woman took the coins and nodded smugly. "I knew you wouldn't take no for an answer."

Despite her stress, Lark found herself smiling back. "You did?"

"Of course. You looked ready to take on the world when you went marching up that hill, didn't you then?"

"I guess I did."

"So what did you think?"

"About what?"

The woman laid down the sewing in her lap. "About him. The master of the inn is quite something, isn't he?"

Lark looked down at her hands. "Yes, he is."

"You'll have nothing to worry about now—relax and have some tea." She pointed to the pot sitting on the hearth. Lark stood to pour some into a worn pottery cup.

The wind blew against the front door and then it burst open. Lark jumped up to close it, but a hand pushed back around the door edge.

"Sorry," the young man said as he pushed his way in, shaking mist from his jacket. It was the man who had questioned her about the south at the inn earlier. "It just started blowing."

"Now look at my floor, son! Did you have to bring the whole storm in with you?"

"It's not a storm, Ma, don't exaggerate." He smiled and shrugged at Lark, then pulled off his oiled cloak and dropped it in a puddle by the fire. "Any supper left?"

"I know the Gentleman fed you up at the inn already—"

"—But, Ma—"

"As if I would let you go hungry. Sit yourself down near the fire and I'll bring it to you."

She bustled over the fire, dishing up what looked like a stew with dumplings in it and handing it to her son. Lark's mouth watered as she smelled the sharp, fishy scent of the hot stew, and she realized she hadn't eaten since morning.

With another smile, Moon dished up a generous bowl of the stew for Lark as well, and then she sat down and took up her sewing, and the lost thread of their conversation. "Now there's an example for you, girl. You'll have no more need to worry about food after this. Why when his father died and I had not a grain of rice in the house, Master Raven just says one day, 'get down to the port in Kÿa'—that's the next village over, you know—and—"

"—and before I could think I had a job on a whaling crew," her son said. "We took three whales last spring and I brought home enough coin to feed us for a year."

"Not to mention the dried whale meat half Rïal ate on for months. That's your Master Raven."

Lark liked the sound of that. "Her" Master Raven. She bent her head over the soup bowl and took a sip of the rich broth while Moon continued.

"Didn't know he had even noticed we was struggling, and there he was, like dropping a gift out of the God's own hand into our laps."

Lark blew on one of the steaming dumplings and asked, "But whaling's rough work, isn't it?"

The boy nodded, his mouth full of his mother's fish dumplings. He took a swallow of tea. "But the money's the best I've ever seen. I'm just working on a fishing net for now. In a couple months I'll head back over there for the season."

"Aren't you afraid?" She pictured the tiny bark coracles on the open sea, rowing up alongside a sperm whale big as a castle. "What if they attack?"

"It's all in surprising 'em. They don't pay attention cause the boats are so small, and then you have to work fast. You shoot arrows into them that have air-filled skins on the end of ropes, so when they dive to get away, they have to drag the air with them. It wears them out. It takes a long time, but eventually they get tired."

Lark bit into a dumpling while the boy described the work. She looked around the little cottage with its warm yellow firelight, and thought of the cold white light of the spermaceti candles that lit the Ariane Mission and the royal palace. She had never thought of the dangerous work it took to light those glorious palaces.

"We have to wait until they come past the northern tip of the isle in spring to go to work again," he finished.

She swallowed the dumpling and tried to picture this slim young man in a life and death battle against the massive whale. "It sounds like rough work."

"It is. But it's the only way for a small boat to go up against a big beast like that. You gotta surprise them and then wear 'em down."

"But to go out to sea—"

He shrugged. "It's where the whales are." He stood up and handed his empty bowl to his mother. "Wake me before dawn, Ma?" He went off somewhere in the back of the cottage and left them alone.

"I guess I'll be off to sleep myself," Lark said. She needed to think. What would she do about Raven?

Moon took her empty bowl from Lark. "You look worried, girl. No need, you know."

Lark stood and brushed her hands over her rough gown. "No need?"

"I've known our Raven for almost fifteen years. He's a good man. He'll give you a fair work. That old Oxen, he's a tough one, but Raven's a good man."

Lark paused. "I'll help you with the dishes," she said.

Over the cracked cups and rough-made pottery bowls Lark broached the subject. "Fifteen years, eh? That's how long you've lived here?"

"Me? No," Moon said. "I've lived here all my life, and my family before me for seven generations. It's Raven who came here from outside."

"Really?" Lark asked innocently. "I wondered...."

Moon splashed the dishrag into the dish of soapy water and

grinned at her. "Of course you wondered, girl. You can see what's in front of you...." She let the sentence dangle there.

Lark waited.

"Handsome, isn't he?" Moon finally said with a twinkle in her eye.

"You think he's handsome?" Lark answered, startled.

"Oh, I know he has the scar, but still, there's something about him. Something special. Didn't you see it?"

"Yes," Lark said softly. "I saw it."

Moon handed her one of the cups to dry. "Like when he got my boy the job on the whaling crew."

Lark thoughtfully ran one finger over the cup's chipped rim. "Yes?"

"He does things like that. Little things that mean a lot to others. He's not so hard a man as he seems. He's quiet, though. Never talks about himself."

Of course not. He couldn't repeat the lies.

"He's never said anything about his background?"

Moon shook her head. "But you know how it is. You hear things about him in the village. And that uncle of his says enough."

"He's not an easy one, that's for sure," Lark said carefully.

"Still, you'll be able to work with them. Master Raven will make sure you're safe now."

"I'm glad of that," Lark said softly, smothering a smile at the irony of the prince keeping the helpless little Ariane girl safe from harm.

"So, about you...?"

Lark looked up. "Me?"

"My son told me you was from the south."

"Yes," Lark said, trying to remember the exact details of her earlier story. "I worked in a kitchen in a noble house before the Var came."

"That explains it." Moon nodded smugly.

"What?"

"The way you have about you. Your manner is different, like you are above us."

Lark felt embarrassed. "I'm sorry. I didn't mean to appear arrogant."

"No," Moon said quickly. "Not arrogant. Different."

Lark looked down at her hands. "I am not different. I am not of high caste."

"Oh, anyone can see that, girl. It is plain you are of good peasant stock. I meant only, there's something—I'm sorry. I didn't mean to make you feel bad."

"I don't feel bad," Lark lied. "I do understand. I am not fully one kind or another. I don't fit."

Moon smiled that broad, open smile at her. "But it's all right, dear. You fit here. You are most welcome with us."

Lark couldn't help smiling back. Yes. She was welcome. What had she said earlier about hating the peasant life? There were some things about it she liked very much indeed.

Moon rubbed her hands on her apron. "Like Master Raven."

"Like him?"

"He's not quite like us, you understand?"

"Yes. Very much so." She tried to think how to ask about that.

"He's not from here," Moon volunteered. "You're curious, aren't you? That's what you want to know about?"

"Yes, I am. Is it that obvious?"

"Well, you'll be working for him, you should know all about it. The story is he worked for a nobleman in the south."

"But surely—?"

"He's no peasant stock, eh? Yeah, but the rumor is he's from, you know, the wrong side of the marriage bed. A bastard that some noble thrown out to fend for himself, you know how they are."

"Yes," Lark said. "I know how the nobles are. So why did he come here?"

"He won't speak of it himself, you understand, but his uncle said they all died in a Var raid, something awful."

Awful was right.

"So his uncle brought him up here to make a new home. Master

Raven himself said to me once he had no friends left where he came from."

"No friends? He said that?" Was that the truth as he believed it? "It's hard to believe he had no one who cared for him," she added awkwardly to cover her shock.

"Aye, but you know how it is. People must look after their own. They'd not have time for an orphaned boy who couldn't put in a full day's work. So here he landed with his uncle."

"You mean Oxen."

"Yes. The old one had saved up enough to buy the inn, so they settled here. And it's been a blessing from God to the village I tell you that."

A blessing from God? All blessings officially came from the nobles' gods, and their worldly symbols, the royal family and the nobles.

The woman looked over her shoulder. Lark followed her gaze and noticed a tiny shrine of the nobles' gods stuck in the corner. The woman looked at it, as if in apology. The shrine was mandatory, but was Moon speaking of something else?.

Lark tentatively made the sign of a triangle in the air.

"Yes." Moon nodded significantly. She echoed the sign.

"But can you say that out loud here? In the south we don't dare."

She laughed. "We don't dare here either, girl. But I can see you ain't one of them nobles. Not like you're going to report me to the prefect."

Lark smiled and looked away into the fire. No, she wouldn't report her for worshipping the peasants' God. But more to the point: "You called Master Raven a blessing from God. In what way?"

Moon rubbed her wet, reddened hands together and thought about it. "He's one of those people who have a light inside of them —you see them every once in a great while. They make things better around them. You ever know someone like that?"

Lark nodded. "I knew someone like that once. But this man, for example...?"

"Well, there's that little boy of his."

"His boy?"

"That little Mouse. Was a slave belonging to some tinker travelling through, and Raven didn't like the way the boy was handled, so he just up and bought him off the man. Raven took him in, though it was a bad year and I think he shorted himself at supper to see the child ate regular."

They sat back down by the hearth. Lark warmed her wet hands while the woman stoked the fire.

"And at the village meetings," Moon continued. "Raven's the one finds a middle ground when the shouting gets out of hand. He's got the level head among the men." Lark pictured him, with that quiet authority, sitting back and watching, listening, observing, then speaking common sense to settle the blustering voices around him.

"We asked him to represent the precinct," Moon continued. "He can talk good, and he has no greed in his heart. We thought maybe he could convince them rich nobles out there not to raise the taxes anymore. But he said no."

"That's too bad."

"He said he wasn't right for the task 'cause he has no leadership ability."

Lark choked, and Moon laughed at her face. "Yes, you see it, too. If he's not a leader I don't know who is."

Lark did indeed 'see it'. Prince Raven could hardly go to Chÿar and count silk cocoons with the other precinct representatives. Here in this remote village he could use that ridiculous story that Oxen was his uncle, but not around those who would know too quickly how out of place he was, and might recognize in the tall, quiet man someone from their own past....

Moon went to a chest over on the wall by the little shrine. She got out a thin woolen blanket and handed it to Lark. "You can bed down right here by the fire, it'll keep you warm enough." She grinned widely. "And if you dream about a certain gentleman in the night, it'll keep you plenty warm, too, I'll bet."

Lark laughed. "I imagine a lot of the local women dream those dreams."

"Of course. But he keeps mostly to himself, now."

"Now?"

"When he was younger—when he was about your age, half a dozen years ago, there had been his wife."

"Wife?" Lark's shock was misinterpreted by the woman.

"Oh, yes. He was married for a few months. As close to happy as I think I ever saw him. but—"

"—But what?" Lark interrupted, shocked out of her humor. "She left him?"

"She died giving birth. A girl. Stillborn."

Lark's mind leaped back to young Mouse, and to Raven, alone on a hill on a Sabbath's eve, thinking perhaps of what might have been.

"He spoke little after that," Moon said quietly. "Though he said to me once—but you don't need to hear it."

Lark felt tears in her eyes. He had lost so much, and now she was blundering into his life to disrupt it again.

She looked up at Moon. "Yes?" she said to her. "Please tell me what he said. I want to know."

Moon looked sorrowful. "He said it was for the best." She shook her head. "His bloodline was cursed to die out for some sin he thought they had committed. I told him it wasn't right to speak so. Nothing a good man like him could have done could earn such a curse."

Lark felt the tears in her eyes, but didn't bother to brush them away. "What did he say to that?"

"He said that he was the last of his family, and 'twas best if his bloodline died with him."

# IV

The iron heels on Lark's heavy peasant boots clicked across the great room's slate floor, echoing throughout the Black Bird Inn. She'd overslept, haunted by dreams of a tall, grieving prince. Now at midday the room was empty, except for one kindly soul....

Dark alleys of Chÿar boasted friendlier faces than the one that glared at her from the far corner. "You're late," Ox grunted from his seat by the hearth.

She sighed, and bowed her head. "I'm sorry, Old Man," she mumbled in her most modest tone. At the rate she was going, she'd be a diplomat yet. Or she'd end up dead, she told herself cheerfully.

"Oxen," the old man muttered.

"What?"

"I said, girl, the name's Oxen. Not 'Old Man.'" It was barely audible, making her step closer to even hear. The old one did not look up. He just kept whittling at a piece of wood. Again he plays with sharp objects, she thought as she watched the gleam of steel bite into the soft stick.

He threw the stick into the fireplace, where it caught light with a sharp crackle. The carving had been a bird, now withering to ash in the flames.

"A raven, eh?" she said, trying out her diplomat skills. "Like this place's namesake?"

Ox pointed wordlessly to a niche in the wall she hadn't noticed before. Another carving, like the one on the front door. An obsidian-eyed raven perched against a fir branch in bas relief. But this was different in setting. This black bird was not a decoration, but a representation of the Gatekeeper, one of the gods of the afterlife in the nobles' religion. A small wooden cup sat on the shelf beneath the carving.

It didn't look well-tended, but the official altar, required of every house in the land, was there. No one could say they hadn't done their duty. She'd seen many like that, mere obedience to the law, while the residents' hearts were elsewhere. From the dust on the old carving and cup, it appeared the nobles' gods received the minimum of attention required to keep this house on the right side of the law. If anyone checked, the gods were properly honored in this house, and only the dust proved how empty that honor was to the peasants who lived here.

She dipped her finger into the empty cup, and touched the finger to her lips in ceremonial respect for the blessings provided by the Gatekeeper. Ox raised an eyebrow. Odd for the peasant Lark to worship the official gods. Of course it was odder still for Lark y Ariane to worship the peasants' God. But she had fought with that contradiction all her life—mostly by pretending it didn't exist. Some day she was afraid she would be forced to choose, to decide once and for all where her own heart lived. But not today. Today she had other concerns.

"I worked in a noble house," she said lamely to explain her action. "They were very strict about protocol."

"It's not my concern what god you waste your time on," Ox said with a snort. "They're all dead to me." He stood and stalked off toward the cookroom without a backward glance. She followed meekly behind, watching his back. Oxen. She didn't remember anyone named Oxen from the royal castle, but that meant nothing. She had spent her time in the kitchen and the dining hall, and on errands to the market. As a slave-child in a castle with hundreds of servants, she had seen little and had known no one.

But Oxen must have been somewhere close to Raven in order to be in a position to become his protector. She watched him stalk ahead, fingering his knife. He was obsessed with security, and with protecting his "nephew." Something in the peasant classes of security, she thought. Something to do with violence and weapons and soldiering, certainly.

He entered the kitchen, then turned back to glare at her as she followed him in. Definitely something involving violence, she decided. It wasn't like he had been employed tending flowers or anything like that.

He pointed to yet another pile of vegetables.

"Surely I chopped enough last eve for a fortnight?" she asked with a smile.

He did not smile back.

The chopping knife stood point down in the wooden counter where she'd left it last night. She took it and began her work. Ox went about his own business in the kitchen without a glance or word in her direction. After much banging of pots and pans, he finally settled at a table opposite her, a large basket of shellfish before him, and that gleaming knife, as always, in his hand. The silence stretched out between them.

"Have you always been a cook?" she asked, though she knew that answer at least. If he had served in the royal kitchen, she would have met him before.

He did not answer.

"Give me a hint, anyway. Have you been a soldier? A silk-weaver? A gardener?"

He looked up at her sharply, then went back to his work.

"You don't like me much, do you, Oxen?"

He shrugged in reply. His hands kept busy inserting the knife point into each clam shell, prying it open, and scooping the sweet flesh into a pot.

"I'm grateful for the work," she said.

"So you've said."

Well, her plan to get him talking wasn't working.

He took his pot of clams to the hearth. Another pot hung on a hook over the fire. He wrapped a cloth around his hands, then removed the hot pot from the hook, and replaced it with the one of clams.

She needed to try another tack. "Is that My Lord Raven's meal?" she asked.

Ox shrugged again, and she took that as affirmation.

She swallowed hard. This might not work, but it was worth a try: "He has no wife, has he?"

Oxen stared at her again at that. "He did once. She died young."

That confirmed what her landlady had said, then. "No companion?" she asked innocently, and found herself truly wondering about the answer. Still your heart, she told herself firmly.

But he did not answer that question. "Is that your game?" he asked. "You set your sights high, girl, if you think you can become mistress of this place."

She set her sights a great deal higher than that, but she merely smiled at the old man. "And if I do set my sights on a man who owns an inn, what harm is there in it? He will decide if he finds me as intriguing as I find him, will he not?"

He turned away from her, muttering something under his breath. He didn't seem to believe her. She wasn't sure why not, since the thought of truly attempting to seduce Lord Raven really did set her pulse pounding.

She watched as he took the lid off the pot he'd just removed from the fire. He brought out a plate, spread steaming rice over it, then used two spoons to carefully lift out the pot's contents and set it on the bed of rice. Fish for Lord Raven's meal. Perfect. A plan emerged from her fog of jumbled thoughts.

"Let me take it to him." That finally made Ox look at her again. "No need, girl."

Oh, yes, there was a need. This might be her last chance to catch him alone before Mouse figured out she was a liar and she had to resort to violence to get some answers.

She winked at Oxen. "Perhaps he'd rather have his meal served by me—"

Ox stopped, pot lid in hand—"Instead of a relic like me?"

She smiled what she hoped was a guileless smile. Lord above, she had no experience at flirtations, but her manner seemed to be enough to convince him of her intentions.

His shoulders dropped and he seemed to relax. "If that's what you're after, you had best try it and be done with it." He handed her the plate. "The sooner I let you try, the sooner he'll set you out on your ear. Give it your best, girl."

She would.

Outside the cookroom she heaved a sigh of relief. That had been more difficult than she had expected. She had never in her life tried to be seductive, and obviously wasn't any good at it. Since she had taken a vow of chastity at the age of five, it was probably a good thing that she had no skill as a courtesan.

She looked down at the plate. A small blue mackeral, studded with herbs, lay gleaming on its bed of rice.

The fish's head pointed toward the left.

She set the plate on a wooden bench in the great room, and carefully picked up the fish, rearranging it so its head pointed toward the right. Then she took it down the far hall toward the sleeping chambers.

One door at the farthest end of the hall stood cracked open, and she could smell the smoke from a pipe coming from inside. But before she faced the man in the far room she wanted to do a little exploring. Other doors opened into the hallway. She quietly stopped at each closed door, and eased it open to peek inside.

One storage space with a dim light wafting in from a tiny window high on the wall. No bars on the window, for it appeared too small for anyone larger than little Mouse to wiggle through, and was at least the height of two men from the ground.

On the opposite side of the hall was a small room lined in reddish slate. She smiled. If a private bathing chamber in a humble inn was not evidence of the innkeeper's noble breeding, she could not imagine what would be: a small windowless room, with a brazier, currently unlit, to heat the pots of water for Lord Raven's bath.

Next was a sleeping chamber, and judging from the musty smell, long disused. Bars on the window. A chest along the far wall—when she eased it open she found it held clothing. She set the plate of fish down and picked up the top gown. Soft green silk, cut generously in the middle for a woman late in pregnancy. The gown had been carefully folded away with sweet herbs for an owner who would never need it again. Touching the soft folds somehow made Raven's loss more real—a wife gone so young; a child, last of her line, never given a chance to live at all. And this after all the earlier tragedy. No wonder Raven spoke of a curse on his family. She picked up the plate of food and left the room to its ghosts.

The next room was a sleeping chamber, sparsely furnished. Again a barred window, and a pallet on the floor. The simple furnishings spoke of the old soldier who slept there within earshot of his master.

The last door, at the end of the hall. She stopped in front of it. Inside she could hear the creaking of the chair. She knocked softly.

She had already come to recognize the accent of the voice that bade "enter" and had to quell, once again, the mixture of fear and anticipation at facing him. She opened the door wide and stepped inside.

———

Raven sat in his bedchamber, staring into the fire, his pipe forgotten in his hand. The fire in the grate was burning low, and the red coals reminded him of another fire, many years ago....

He banished the thought. Was Oxen right, or was Lark? Was it right for the prince to stay hidden when others were suffering? But how could he help, when the peasants had been the ones who murdered his family, left their bodies in the charred rubble of the palace, and even all these years later, would kill him on sight?

He heard the door open, and Lark stepped inside, shutting the door behind her. He looked up. Lark was standing before him, words clearly at the tip of her tongue fighting to get out. And he knew, with all his soul, that whatever she had to say would make him miserable, would ruin what little bit of peace he had managed to carve out for himself.

He nodded a cool greeting.

"Your meal is ready, Sir." She set the plate on the table next to him, then stood back, silent, watching.

He ignored the plate for a moment, once again taken aback by her presence. She fairly bristled with energy, and yet again he was struck by that sense of familiarity. They stared at each other for a moment.

"Why are you here, Lark?" he finally asked.

She raised an eyebrow. "Why, to bring you your meal, Sir."

"That's not what I mean and you know it. Why are you in Rïal? What brought you here?—and don't start up with that ridiculous story of ten-foot-tall Var marauders again."

She said nothing, but looked down at the plate on the table.

He looked down at the plate, then at her, shocked at her audacity. This could not be happening, not after all these years. He felt a horror wash over him, and tried to hide it.

He carefully picked up the fish, reversing it on the plate.

"Why do you do that?" she asked innocently. Could she possibly be that stupid?

"That is how you serve royalty," he said quietly. "Facing toward the Afterlife. It is not appropriate for anyone else to look toward the gods, even symbolically. I thought you'd done scullery work before."

"That was how I was taught to serve my master."

"The only place you serve fish facing so is in the house of the king."

She said nothing, but just stared pointedly at him. Was that why she looked familiar? Had she served in the palace? But she was no meek servant—how could he not remember someone as audacious as her?

He chuckled. "Is that what you think?" He tried to make light of it. This really was happening. The peasant assassins had found him.

He glanced toward the corner, where his scabbard stood propped.

She was on her knees next to him. "I am no threat to you, Your Grace." She looked up into his face. "Do you not remember me? I was always called Lark, but far more often, just Girl."

Suddenly it came to him. Put aside her brash manner, put aside her lithe body and physical grace, and there was a lost little girl at the heart of her. Of course. It was her eyes he remembered. Girl, fetch the wine. Girl, pick that up. Girl, get out of the way. A starving slave-child of the lowest caste, all huge eyes and gaunt limbs. Frightened, alone, working until she dropped and then ignored until more work was needed by her "betters."

"You were tiny," he whispered. "You couldn't have been more than five years old."

"Yes, My Prince." She sighed. "I have searched so long for you."

So she was in league with the peasant assassins. Given her past, how could he blame her for hating the royal family. "But I'm no threat to you, or to your people, Lark."

She seemed startled by that. "Threat? Your Grace, you are our only hope. We need you."

"Need me? Why?"

"Don't you understand, Your Grace? Someone has to lead the people. Someone has to give them hope. There are still ceremonies held at the tombs in Chÿar, where the whole city grieves for you."

He pulled back from her. She could not be serious. He was not the boy prince any longer. "Those are empty rituals put on by the Ariane to confirm their status as stewards. They must make those gestures to show they are holding the kingdom for the missing king, so no one questions their right to rule. It means nothing, Lark. The rituals are about convincing the people to pay their taxes on time, not about any genuine desire for a change in power. The king is gone. The Ariane can protect the people as well as the royal family ever did."

"That's not the point."

"Isn't it, Lark? You want a leader, but the leader of the Ariane holds the throne—"

"—Awaiting your return, Your Grace. The Lady Willow holds the throne for the king during the interregnum. We don't need a substitute, we need the king himself, Your Grace."

His grace. He hated the term. "I am not 'Your Grace.' I am Raven, an innkeeper, and I want to be left alone."

"But the people of the Silver Isle need a leader. I spoke what I believed in the hall last night."

"And I spoke what I believed, Lark. Any man who believes in the idealistic words of the last prince is a fool."

"But your Martyrsday speech...." She trailed off, tears in her eyes.

The Martyrsday speech. It seemed almost a memory from another life: A man-child, adolescent voice cracking with emotion, trembling before the glowering tower of a man that was his sire. Empty, pointless words spoken in a futile attempt to save the lives of condemmed peasants: *My father-king, does that shepherd's crook you hold serve only as a resting place for your sapphires and diamonds? Or can your humble subjects—this young son among them—look to you with hope and pride as a shepherd to guide us out of this darkness wrought of poverty and superstition?*

He tried not to cringe at the naïveté. It was from another life, a life destroyed in a blaze of violence and flame fifteen years ago. Now the peasants of the Silver Isle were lost. They labored until they were exhausted, paid all they made in taxes to keep the rich in luxury, and then ended up either dying young from overwork or as fodder for the barbarian hordes streaming across the sea toward their defenseless island.

It was not his fight anymore. He had been a fool to think it ever had been.

"What do you want of me? I cannot change the way things have always been, especially not now. I am damaged. I cannot lead battles like this. And I am in no shape to battle my own people."

"Why not, Your Grace?"

"What do you want? A lost prince come back from the dead to fulfill some legendary role as savior-king? A figurehead standing on top of a mountain with my cloak billowing picturesquely in the breeze, making speeches to inspire you in your hopeless battle against an undefeatable enemy? I'm not good at that sort of thing."

A faint smile. "You're doing all right so far, Your Grace."

He was not amused. "Let your prayers to your peasant God comfort you in your delusions. I want no part of your charade."

Now it was her turn to be angry. She stood before him, hands fisted in frustration and glaring down at him. "Our 'delusions' are no worse than your jug of wine, Your Grace. They give us strength to arise another day. Who's to say which is the worse escape? You sit here and smoke your pipe and drink your wine while people starve in the countryside." There was the fiery girl of last night. How had a meek slave child become this firebrand? He shook himself free of the spell of her passion.

"It is beyond my control," he said firmly.

"If it's beyond yours, it's beyond anyone's. If not you, then who, My Prince?"

He looked away. Those were the very words he had been telling himself since yesterday—hell, he had been telling himself that all his life. But who was she to say this to him?

She spoke again, but more softly now: "Is this who you are meant to be? Is this your highest calling, to run this inn and serve food to the needy?"

"I am helping this village," he whispered, knowing what an inadequate answer that was.

"It's not enough, Your Grace. It is not enough for a man who can save the world to save a few."

That cut like a knife into his soul. He turned his head away. "But they will not accept the king. The peasants who murdered the royal family will never accept him."

"They must be made to accept him."

He faced her again. This he knew was untrue. "At what cost must they be forced, Lark? Have you seen the Ariane in action? Yes, they can subdue a horde of peasants, but how many people will die to impose an unwanted king on the masses? How many lives would it cost to restore the crown? So many have already died. So many are gone. Everyone in the royal household—" He stopped there as it struck him. Why was Lark alive? All of the royal household had been murdered in the assassination of the royal family. How had this little child escaped?

"I remember the cost, Your Grace," she said softly, and he saw the pain in her eyes. Yes, she had been there. She had seen the mass murder of innocents. Somehow she had escaped, like he had, but it had scarred her, too.

"It is over, Lark," he said quietly. "An unsteady peace is better than more class warfare. Too many have died for this cause. We have to let the past go. Let the Ariane leader serve as best she can, and you peasants must make the best of your lives. Any other course will lead us all to ruin."

She stood there, straight and tall, and looked down on him with what seemed like contempt. "And you are satisfied with that?"

He looked away, not wanting to face her scorn. "It is the most rational choice. We can't always have the ideal, Lark."

"I will not accept that." She looked down on him, simmering with anger.

"You 'will not'? What answer will you accept from me, girl?"

"You must come back with me to Chÿar, to take your place as king, and bring peace and prosperity to the Silver Isle." She said this outrageous statement matter-of-factly, as if it were actually possible to do just that.

"Is that all?" He brought his cup of wine to his lips, thought better of it, then set it down. "I will not take the throne of the Silver Isle. It does not belong to me."

"Then to whom, Your Grace? If you had been to the city, you would see how frightened the people are—and throughout the countryside where I've traveled, they do not know what to do. If they had someone to lead them, someone to give them hope...."

"I cannot be that hope."

"You must."

"I must?" His voice was icy. "I also said what I believed last night."

"That the king answers to no one but himself? You cannot mean that. Prince Raven spoke of the king's duty to be a shepherd for his people—"

"—Prince Raven was a naïve fool. I believe that it would not matter if there were a king on the throne of the Silver Isle. I believe we are doomed, girl."

"We are not doomed!" She was shouting now. "How can you say this when so many are counting on you? It is all they live for. The Ariane have promised the people a king will return someday. We have searched for years for you."

"We? You speak for the Ariane? They sent a slave to fetch me to fulfill their empty promises?"

She seemed to bristle at that. "I am one of the few who would know you by sight, My Prince."

"I am not your prince, girl. And I am not the boy I was fifteen years ago. I am just an innkeeper, trying to live out my life in peace."

The door swung open with a bang. Oxen stood in the entrance, cleaver in hand. "I heard raised voices, Sir."

Just like Ox to step in. He had been right about the girl. She was dangerous. But if he told Oxen that she knew the truth about him, the old man would kill her where she stood. He would not have more blood on his hands. "Yes, you did hear voices," he said. "Lark was just telling me she's leaving us, Ox. Will you escort her to the gate and lock it behind her?"

"With pleasure, Sir."

Raven stood up. He leaned in close to Lark, and took her by the shoulders to give her the formal kiss of parting. But instead of a kiss, he whispered in her ear so Ox would not hear: "You must go, Lark. If you speak the truth, and you are loyal to what you think I am, you will not tell anyone of this. I am not the boy you remember. You must let it go."

She bowed, then silently followed Ox out, leaving him alone with his cold supper and his thoughts.

Lark paused in the shadow of the barn's overhanging roof. It was just past moonrise. Rain poured down, turning the pathways to muck.

Inside the barn she sensed the sheep stirring, and the odor of animals was overwhelming to her heightened senses. No horses in there. Good. That would delay anyone who felt like being brave and going for help.

It was warm in there, she imagined, but her Ariane cloak kept her warm enough outside. If her doeskin boots didn't have a hole in them she would hardly mind the rain at all. She should have had them repaired while she was in Rïal, but it was too late to think of it now, and she was not about to go back to wearing the heavy-soled peasant boots that had weighed her down these last few days.

The barn was only a few paces from the Black Bird Inn, and she watched the inn's windows for a while, looking for signs of life. Nothing. Steady breathing from several windows confirmed what the darkened windows implied. The inn's three occupants were all asleep.

There was a dark slit high up on the inn's wall, marking the second clerestory window from the large chimney of the great room's west hearth. That was her target. The weak link in the inn's carefully thought-out defenses.

The one inside would not stop her from completing her task.

She drew her sword and stepped out into the rain.

It was quick work to flow up the side of the building's rough rock exterior and through the window. She dropped to the floor, her suede-soled Ariane boots making no sound on the tiled floor.

Quickly she entered the next room. The sleeper was on his side, facing toward the wall.

One quick thrust of the blade, and it would be over.

But that wasn't the plan. She pulled out the cloth strips she had wound around her wrist. She had her short knife to his throat and a cloth around his mouth before he could move.

Old Oxen's eyes popped open, gleaming in the dark.

He was fast, much quicker than she had expected from the old one, and she was forced to quickly throw him to the ground. He took a small table down with him, and she realized he was trying to make as much noise as possible.

She put her sword to his throat. "I don't want to kill you, Old One," she whispered fiercely. "Don't force me to."

His eyes took in her cloak and sword, and he lay back as the realization of what she was hit him.

"Yes, you cannot win against me. Don't make me change my mind about sparing you."

She bound him using the one-handed knot-tying technique Lotus had taught her last winter. When she was done she stood. He could not move or speak, but he could still glare at her. She smiled down at him.

"You have served your master well, Old Man. Now it is my turn."

---

Fire. The horrific smell of burning flesh, and the knowledge that the flesh was his own family.

His leg was broken, and blood ran down his face. He couldn't see, which was just as well, as he lay prone next to the flames—it was best not to see what was there so close by.

Father, that stubborn, hateful man.

Kestrel, Raven's older brother, just like Father, a born leader, uncompromising and sure of himself.

All the servants of the royal household, innocent casualties of the political tsunami destroying them all.

God only knew what else lay in the pile of burning flesh he had just pushed aside in his desperate attempt to get away from the heat.

The only grace was that Mother was already dead and would never know what disaster her death had set in motion.

There were no cries in the room. Just an eerie roar from the flames, hissing as they grew, feeding on their gruesome fuel. He was locked in this scalding room with death. Only he was alive in here. If only he had not awoken. A few seconds more of unconsciousness and he would never have known what had happened.

He reached out and felt the stone wall of the Griffon palace, the royal family's shelter from the world outside, and now, fittingly, their tomb. The walls around him felt solid, and he could see nothing. He curled up his battered body as best he could in the corner farthest from the fire.

The crackling was deafening now. The building itself might crack soon in this heat. Outside he thought he heard voices shouting, some distance away.

The end would come soon now.

Then old Ox was there, dragging his broken body toward some draft of fresh air, and muttering all the while. "By God, My Prince, you're awake! We must hurry—"

"Don't leave me, Oxen."

"Never, Your Grace—My King."

"Not that. Not ever." How could he take the crown won through his family's death?

"We have to get you out of here, Your Grace—Sir. Lean on me, Lord Raven." The raw croak of Ox's voice echoed in his ears. He felt the old man tugging on his body and shouting above the sickening roar and smoke of the fire: "Hurry, Sir. If they come back—"

He awoke in sweat, shaking. He could almost swear the scent of death lingered on him. It had been a long time since he had dreamed like that. Not long enough. He wiped his hand across his face. None of this mattered anymore. No one else knew, and that servant girl could do nothing to him.

He lay back against his pallet, and willed himself back to sleep. But a movement by the hearth made him sit up again.

Lark stepped out of the shadow and stood over him, cloaked in glittering Ariane silver, and holding a gleaming sword.

"Get up, Raven yr Griffon," she said. "It's time for you to come home."

Next:

## *Lark's Quest: The Secret*

*In the second novella, Lark has found Raven yr Griffon, the young prince who escaped the massacre of the royal family fifteen years ago. But this is only the beginning of the story. For Raven has no intention of returning to the throne, and Lark will have to make decisions that will affect the future of the Silver Isle in ways she never imagined. Her return to the city doesn't go as planned, and she encounters both friends and enemies in her quest to make the lost prince the king of the Silver Isle.*

*Meanwhile, Raven's friends Oxen and little Mouse are not going to give up so easily. They are soon on the march to protect their beloved friend from Lark's plot at any cost.*

10% of the earnings from each of Barbara Cool Lee's books is donated to charity. The charity for the *Deeds of the Ariane Novellas* is the Second Harvest Food Bank, http://www.thefoodbank.org. A complete list of charities receiving donations is kept updated at http://www.BarbaraCoolLee.com.